CHRISTMAS IN JULY

A GARLAND HOLIDAY ROMANCE

LUCINDA RACE
MADDIE JAMES

TWO BOOTS PUBLISHING

Christmas In July

Lucinda Race
Maddie James

Christmas in July: A Garland Holiday Romance
eBook ISBN: 978-1-62237-536-3

Editor: Kimberly Dawn
Cover Art: Jacobs Ink, LLC

This is a work of fiction. Characters, settings, names, and occurrences are a product of the authors' imaginations and bear no resemblance to any actual person, living or dead, places or settings, and/or occurrences. Any incidences of resemblance are purely coincidental.

Two Boots Publishing
June 2022

AUTHOR'S NOTE

Author's Notes

From Lucinda Race

Hi and welcome to my world of romance with a touch of magic. I hope you fall in love with my characters as much as I do. So, turn the page and fall in love again.

If you'd like to stay in touch, please join my Newsletter. I release it twice per month with tidbits, recipes and occasionally a special gift just for my readers so sign up here: **https://lucindarace.com/newsletter/** and there's a free book when you join!

Happy reading...

From Maddie James

There's nothing in this world I love better than a holiday romance story—unless it would be chocolate. Or perhaps flirty kisses under the mistletoe with my sweetheart. Or maybe all the above! Do I have to choose?

I'm so excited to share *Christmas in July* with you. I hope you love it and want to read more in my fictional worlds. To keep up with my book news, feel free to sign up for my ***VIP Insider Newsletter*** and grab your free gift while you are at it! Just click here to get started: **https://maddiejamesbooks.com/pages/newsletter**

Love, Maddie

CHRISTMAS IN JULY

Sylvia Moore returns to Garland during the annual Christmas in July festival, hoping to land the New England location for a new Christmas romance movie. She knows the town will award only one filming permit a year, but is confident the deal's in Santa's bag.

After all, she's the hometown girl with the hometown advantage.

But her rival, Chase Ellis, is also in town, and he's out to grab the Garland location for a movie, too, working the locals and smooth-talking the town council. This is a familiar snowy path and Sylvia ponders whether to confront or avoid him. They're both staying at Holly Hill Inn, so avoiding him—and his molten chocolate brown eyes—is impossible.

Then Chase proposes a sweet as Christmas candy deal. When that falls through, Sylvia counters with a deal of her own.

Both know their reputations and careers are on the line. Sylvia assures her boss the contract is in her Christmas stocking. Chase knows if he loses, he risks future jobs for his newly formed company. And if that isn't enough, the competition takes on an unexpected twist when the two sneak kisses that could scorch even the hottest of days during the Christmas in July festival.

CHAPTER ONE

Sylvia parked on the circular driveway in front of Holly Hill Inn, and it was a welcome sight. From the holly berry bushes flanking the brick walkway to the deep-red painted clapboards and bright-white trim, the front porch beckoned visitors to relax from the day's heat. Sylvia checked her hair and makeup in the car mirror, which remained flawless despite the July humidity, before going inside.

It had been years since she'd been back in New England after relocating to Los Angeles. The only thing she wanted was a successful business trip, and maybe to show everyone she had fulfilled her dream of becoming a sought-after location manager for films, and that she owned a thriving business.

She'd decided to stay at Holly Hill Inn in Charmington, a small town just a stone's throw away from her hometown of Garland, because while she was happy to be back home, landing the location contract was her priority. She didn't need to get caught up in small town drama for the few days she'd be in town.

So, Charmington was safe. Close enough, but far enough away, too.

With her laptop case resting on top of her roller bag, she walked up the path to the front door. Her footsteps slowed, and she blinked. What the heck was Chase Ellis doing standing on the porch? Was it possible he was here scouting locations for a new holiday film? It couldn't be a coincidence, could it? She thought of that line from *Casablanca*. 'Of all the gin joints…'

Had drama followed her to Holly Hill Inn, anyway?

He glanced her way but either didn't want to or just plain didn't recognize her behind the dark sunglasses. It's not like they were good friends, but more like rivals, always competing for the best films to work on. As he grew closer, she looked away to avoid him altogether. She couldn't help but inhale the scent of his cologne. Bleu de Chanel, the citrus combined with sandalwood and cedar, was going to stick with her long after he got in his car. Holding her breath, she glanced toward him as he walked away until he paused and half turned in her direction.

"Sylvia Moore." He walked back to where her feet were cemented to the walkway.

His smile lit up his dark eyes and played across his full lips. She had a fleeting thought about what his scruff of a beard would feel like, and her fingers itched to brush back the lock of dark hair that partially dipped over one eye.

"Chase Ellis. This is a surprise." She didn't extend her hand as if they were friends greeting each other.

"What are you doing in Garland?" he asked.

He was casually dressed in jeans and a body-clinging black tee shirt, which did nothing to hide his six-pack abs. Her mouth went dry. He was much better-looking up close, and his cologne wrapped around her like a lover's embrace.

"I could ask you the same thing." She popped her hand on a hip and thought about how they were dressed very differently. When she wasn't working scouting film locations, she loved her designer labels, even if she shopped for them at a consignment shop. There was nothing wrong with being a bargain hunter.

With a smirk in his eyes, he said, "I asked you first."

"I'm just visiting, and you?" She pushed her sunglasses to the top of her head and watched as his facial expression never changed.

He quirked a brow. "Just passing through and thought Garland was charming. I decided to stay a night or two, soak up the local color and all."

Not that Sylvia believed him. Like her, he had to be working on a new project, but she wouldn't come right out and ask him. "Well, make sure you stop by The Evergreen. My friend Krissy just opened up the diner, and I'm sure it's fabulous."

He tapped his finger on his brow. "Thanks for the tip. I'll see ya around."

Sylvia watched as he strolled away, as though it hadn't bothered him at all to run into her. But he had to be wondering the same thing; what was she really doing in town? Not that she'd tell him she was looking for a location for a new Christmas rom-com. When she was asked to join the preproduction team, she knew Garland was the only place to film it. This was a very special town, and it had everything the script called for, right down to the gazebo in the town square and prerequisite Christmas tree farm on the outskirts. Surely, he couldn't be scouting. That would just ruin everything. Who knew if the town council would give permission for two film crews to come to town in a short time span?

She put her sunglasses back on and strode to the large wooden door. It was time to get checked in and start scouting for locations. There was no way she'd let Chase scoop her in her hometown.

Sylvia drove around for the next hour, absorbing the sights and realizing just how much she had missed home. Not much had changed. Kitty's Knittery was across from the gazebo in the town park, and the florist, Pam's Petals, was thriving on Main Street. Even the community center looked exactly the same. Her parents moved to the Carolinas, so now that's where she went for holidays, but Garland tugged at her heart. She caught sight of the bright carved sign for The Evergreen and parked out front. She might as well get a bite to eat and say hello to Krissy. It had been too long, and it was time to catch up, and who knows, maybe the interior of Evergreen's would be ideal for some shots.

When she walked in with her heels clicking on the tile floor, it took a moment for her eyes to adjust from the bright sun to the interior lighting. She spotted her old friend Krissy, and her smile widened when she recognized Sylvia.

She hurried across the diner and drew Sylvia in for a squeeze. "Why didn't you call and tell me you were coming? It's been what two, three years since we saw each other in Minnesota?"

Sylvia hugged her tightly, happy to see that sunny smile light up her blue eyes. "How could I miss your grand reopening? So glad your Christmas pop-up restaurant experiment was a success. Looks like the move to Garland was a good choice for you, and is Katie happy too?"

At the mention of Krissy's daughter, her smile broadened. "She loves it here, so thank you for encouraging me to check out the town. But what are you doing here, business or pleasure?"

Sylvia glanced around the diner, and that's when she saw him sitting at a corner table, sipping coffee and reading the newspaper. He seemed to be completely unaware, blending in with the locals. As if Chase could blend, with his dark hair and eyes and the scruff of a beard. Her heart rate kicked up, and she forced herself to turn away.

Krissy asked, "Do you know that guy? He's been around this time over the last couple of days. He doesn't talk much, but he's a good tipper."

Without looking at him, Sylvia said, "I know who he is. We work in the same industry." She glanced over her shoulder. "Could I get a coffee and pastry to go? I have an appointment, but I'll stop back later."

Krissy's brow arched and she pursed her lips. "Sure." She glanced at Chase and back to Sylvia. "He leaves by three."

"Um, yeah, sure." With a huge smile plastered on her face, she gave Krissy a quick hug with the promise to be back later. She hitched up her shoulder bag and left the diner without her coffee or a backward glance.

Once outside, she placed a hand over her tummy and took a few deep breaths to calm her fluttering pulse. How on earth could simply being in the same room as Chase give her this kind of reaction? She squared her shoulders and strode off toward town hall. What would it take to gain approval and permits to start filming in September? The gazebo in the town square along with several private properties were perfect for the fall-themed movie.

Standing outside the town hall, Sylvia read the guidelines and the approval process. She needed to submit a letter of intent with the scope of filming, where she wanted to film, duration of filming, and if any roads would be closed. Then submit it to the town manager, and best-case scenario, granted approval within a week or two.

"Hey."

Sylvia jumped as a deep male voice spoke softly. "Chase, what are you doing here?" She dropped her hand by her side so the paperwork wouldn't be on display.

"Same as you, I suspect. Checking to see what the process is for getting permits to film."

His deep voice and the scent of his cologne drove her almost mute. She looked away from him. "I don't know what you're talking about."

He arched a brow as if daring her to skirt the truth. "You're not in town to scout locations for a movie you've been contracted to work on?"

She wasn't about to tell him anything, even though they couldn't be working in the same town at the same time; that was way too close for comfort. "What are you doing here?" Would he stop asking her questions?

He dipped her head and gave her a heart-stopping smile that also implied two could play her game. "I told you. I'm just driving through and decided to take a couple of days and relax."

Okay, so he *was* going to keep this going. She gave a curt nod. "I'm just visiting and catching up with old friends."

He took a step back and swept his arm toward where she had parked her rental car. "Then I won't keep you."

Was he dismissing her so he could take care of business inside? Surely she would not let him get his letter of interest in before her. Sylvia jerked her thumb toward the oversized door to the town hall and then down the street. "I'm going in there, so I guess you'd better get going that way."

She marched to the door, and Chase was half a step behind her until he reached around her and pulled open the door. "After you."

"Chase, are you kidding me?" She stomped in the door and went straight to the desk of the town clerk. She could feel him watching her, and it wouldn't surprise her if he had a smirk on that handsome face of his.

She gave the woman behind the counter a pleasant smile. "Would it be possible to provide a handwritten letter of intent for filming in several areas around Garland?"

"All it takes is being able to read it, and good news for you if you get it in today. The select board is meeting in two days, so you'll get a quick response."

"Would you possibly have some paper?" She looked over her shoulder at Chase, who was patiently waiting his turn at the desk. The clerk handed her several sheets of copy paper and a pen.

"Be as detailed as possible and make sure to include your contact information." She pointed to a wooden bench against the far wall. "You can have a seat over there while I wait on the gentleman behind you."

Inwardly, she groaned but smiled and thanked the woman before moving away.

Chase stepped up to the window, and Sylvia didn't attempt to hide her curiosity.

"Hi, Sue." He withdrew an envelope from his back pocket. "Can you see this goes before the select board too?" He glanced at Sylvia and gave her a saucy wink and then looked back at the clerk. "And I sure do appreciate your help getting this all squared away."

"Chase, it was my pleasure." She took the envelope and gave him a warm smile. It was easy to see that she appreciated the man's good looks. Sylvia dipped her head and studied the blank paper in front of her.

He crossed the small lobby and bent over, saying for her ears alone, "Good luck with your papers, hon, and maybe I'll see you around town. And for the record, the next time you stop by The Evergreen, you should join me for coffee."

CHAPTER TWO

Grinning to himself, Chase Ellis turned and exited the town hall. The expressions traveling over Sylvia Moore's face the past few minutes were priceless. He wished he'd had his camera handy, and the guts to snap a picture of her, but he didn't want to totally irritate his competition.

Yet.

Still, her soft features were a tad amusing—the surprised roundness of her hazel eyes, the hint of question and disbelief showing in them. Her slack mouth shaped into a pouty—and if he were noticing—shapely pucker. Basically, an aura of conflict and confusion summed up her demeanor.

Gotcha, Sylvia Moore!

He'd one-upped her, and she knew it. And that had tossed her off her game. Momentarily. He didn't underestimate her. Not by a long shot.

Snickering and mentally high-fiving himself, he crossed the town square to where he'd parked his rented SUV and pondered that thought. Keeping her off her game was exactly his game plan.

He'd known she'd land in Garland eventually, and he'd done his homework.

While he drove back to Holly Hill Inn, his brain wandered over the past few days. When Signet approached him about scouting the perfect location for their next *Charmed Romance* Christmas movie, he'd jumped at the chance. He preferred working for networks, rather than a major film company—although he wouldn't let one pass by if it came his way—because the work was steady. Network streaming, for both movies and series, had seriously increased his revenue since he'd bitten the bullet and opened his own company last year.

He loved flying solo, in business and in life. That's just how he rolled. Business was going so well right now, he'd probably have to break down and hire an assistant soon.

"Find the most charming, Christmasy New England village you can," Bea Cooper had told him. Bea was the director of the film. They'd worked together before, on another small-town romance series for *Charmed* last year. "I need a gazebo and an old-fashioned hardware store and a diner. Don't forget a pond and a Christmas tree farm. Oh, and a bed-and-breakfast of some sort. You know the type of setting *Charmed* is known for. This place must ooze tinsel and holly and sweat pine resin and maple syrup. You get me, right?"

He so got her.

So much so that she'd loved the preliminaries and photos he'd sent her two days ago. Just that morning, Bea had given him the go-ahead to move forward, submit paperwork, and negotiate fees. They had a system, and he knew where he could go and where he couldn't. There were still logistics to be worked out—that was a given—but he was feeling darned good about himself and the prospect of nailing this one.

Competition for Christmas movie locations was stiff this time of year. And he knew he needed to move quickly. Once a town had committed to a movie, they were sometimes reluctant to consider a second in the same time frame. It would all depend on the powers-that-be in the town who made the decisions.

His New England research had landed him in Garland the weekend before. That's when he had discovered the newly opened diner called The Evergreen. And that's when he also learned that Sylvia Moore was a homespun, hometown Garland girl.

That owner of The Evergreen? Krissy? She liked to talk.

"Oh, so you're a location scout?" She'd asked when he'd shared why he was in Garland. "What a coincidence! My friend, Sylvia, is a location scout too."

What were the odds there was more than one Sylvia who worked in his profession? "Not Sylvia Moore, by any chance?"

"Yes! One and the same. Do you know her? She lives in LA, too."

Like everyone in LA knew each other. Typical small-town thinking. However, in this case…

"Did you know she's from Garland?"

He didn't. And that tidbit of knowledge was a goldmine.

Thank you, Ms. Krissy.

To some, that information may have presented a challenge. Some scouts might even move on after learning that. How do you defeat the hometown girl on her own turf? But to Chase, that knowledge was power and a definite advantage. Plus, he could never resist a challenge.

Game on, Sylvia Moore. Game on.

"I feel like wetting a line in the pond. Want to join me, Chase? I'll even bring a few ice-cold brewskis."

Chase eyed Dylan Hall, co-owner of Holly Hill Inn. His wife, Kat, ran the place. He stood in the inn's kitchen, having come downstairs for a bottle of water. Dinner was over for the Hall family, and Kat was cleaning up.

"That's mighty tempting, Dylan. You want company?"

"Always. This time of evening is a perfect time to chill. Besides, it was damn hot today, and a cold beer sounds good."

"I'll second that."

"Great. I'm heading out back. I'll meet you on the dock in ten minutes with poles and whatnot. See you in a few."

"Want me to bring anything?" Chase called out.

"Nada. Got it covered."

Well, all right then. Chase stood and glanced at Kat. "Fishing is good for him," she said, bending to load the dishwasher.

"Oh?"

Kat stood and faced Chase. "Yes. His job is stressful. Thanks for going with him. You didn't have to." She smiled.

"He had me at brewski." Chase glanced at the counter. A flyer for the annual Christmas in July festivities caught his eye. He picked it up.

"Going to any of the events this week?" Kat asked.

"Maybe. Not sure." He perused the flyer. "Looks like a lot going on."

"Always is, this time of year. The proceeds go toward funding Christmas Week in December in town, with a large percentage also going to the community center this year."

"Sounds like a worthy cause."

"It is."

Chase read through the rest of the flyer. "Mind if I keep this?" He looked at Kat. "I may want to get some additional pictures for the film director. By the way, she loved the images I sent of Holly Hill Inn, so all we need now is the town council approval, and then we can sign the contract."

Kat grinned wide and bounced a little. "Oh, my goodness! That's great to hear, Chase. And good luck!"

A door slammed at the front of the house, grabbing Kat's attention. "Expecting guests. Better see if that's them. Enjoy the dock and the pond." She wiped her hands on a dishtowel and headed toward the lobby.

"Will do, Kat."

Chase exited the back door and strolled down a small hill toward the dock. The day had been sweltering, but now, a cool breeze blew in off the pond. Actually, to him, the body of water seemed more like a small lake.

Dylan walked ahead carrying poles and a cooler. He followed the dock out to a small gazebo built over the water. The far end of the structure was open, no railing, and Dylan set his gear down there. Chase joined him at the gazebo.

"I'm going to park these here." Dylan looked up. "Sorry to say I can't stay. I just got a text, and need to make a call. Not how I was intending to spend my evening, but it comes with the territory. Help yourself to the poles, bait, beer, view..."

Chase nodded. "Thanks, man. Sorry about your evening."

"No worries. It's what I do."

"And what is that, if you don't mind my asking?" He thought about what Kat said a few minutes ago.

Dylan eyed him. "Special forces. We don't talk about it much around here, especially with the locals. Seal Team. I'm home on leave for a few weeks, but..." His phone buzzed again. Dylan glanced at it. "Gotta go." He headed down the dock, then turned. "Hey, there's a super-sized bass in that pond. I've named him Henry. If you catch him, you have to put him back. He's mine!"

Chase gave Dylan a quick salute and turned back to the gear.

A quiet evening in the gazebo on the lake with beer might not be a bad thing. He pulled up a wooden bench, chose a pole, found the bait, popped a top on the beer, and had at it.

Several minutes later, the water lapping at the dock lulling him into a drowsy state of being, he thought he heard footsteps behind him.

"Of all the nerve, Chase Ellis."

He grinned before he turned around, then gave her a serious face. "Why, Sylvia Moore. It's you."

"Oh, don't give me that innocent look." She pulled up another bench and sat across from him. "What are you doing here, Chase? Seriously."

He casually fiddled with his pole, winding the reel a little. "Fishing."

"I mean in Garland."

"Working." He stared at her.

She rolled those pretty hazel eyes of hers. "I know that. I have a proposition for you."

Now this is getting interesting. Chase scooted his bench to square himself in front of her, giving her his full attention. "I'm all ears."

Her gaze narrowed. "Garland is mine, Chase. You need to withdraw your paperwork."

He feigned consideration. "No."

"No?"

"That's right. No. I'm not withdrawing anything."

"But this is my town."

"Really? Do you live here? Where is that sign at the end of town that says, Welcome to Sylvia Moore's Garland?" He reeled in his line and set the pole aside, giving her a moment for a comeback. One never came.

She simply glared.

"Earth to Sylvia. You still with me, darlin'?"

"I'm not your darlin'. And don't you know women don't like to be called endearments like that in the workplace? Chase, you need to up your game. Get a little professionalism about you."

He snickered and ignored all that. "Sylvia Moore," he started, watching her eyes. "First, this isn't the workplace. It's a gazebo on a pond in the middle of the woods in New England. And second, I have a job to do here, and I intend to keep doing it. I'm not withdrawing any paperwork. By the way, you mentioned a proposition. I've yet to hear one."

"Oh." She glanced off and stared toward the back of the inn. "Right."

"Well?"

Slowly, she rotated back, her gaze pinning him to the spot. "Here's the deal. You back out of Garland, and I'll back out of the next one."

Chase lowered his gaze and chuckled. "Sylvia Moore, that is so lame."

"I think that's perfectly reasonable!" Her back shot up, ramrod straight.

"Next one? How do we even know there will be a next one?"

She stood. "Chase, we seem to travel in the same circles here. We've both been after small-town romance, or mystery sets for the past year or longer. There is bound to be a next time."

Chase still sat, looking up at her. Her scrunched brow and arms crossed tightly over her chest told him she was worried. At least a little. Something more was at stake. Reaching into the cooler, he pulled out a cold brew, popped the top, and handed it to her. "Sylvia Moore? You are way too stressed. Have a beer."

Her mouth puckered. Then she took a deep breath and let it out. "I don't drink beer."

"Wine?"

"Well, yes."

"Sorry, fresh out." He set the can aside. "You okay?"

"Perfectly fine." Her chin tilted up.

"Have a seat and let's talk about this. I'm sure there is room for two movies in Garland over the next few months. We can work it out."

But she didn't sit. "No. We can't."

"Why?"

"I have it on good authority that Garland will only consider one movie per year. The last time two movies filmed in the town in the same year, the town businesses lost money. Too much downtime for shop owners. The Chamber of Commerce—while agreeing that a movie in Garland is a great draw and nicely filled the town's coffers—threw a fit, supposedly, because of lost revenue to small business owners. So, Mr. Ellis, I'm asking you nicely. Pull your paperwork, please. I need to land this one."

"Why?"

"Because it would be mighty embarrassing if I didn't."

"Seeing that you are the hometown girl and all."

"You knew that?"

"Your friend talks."

"Krissy?"

"Mm-hmm. That's the one."

"I need this job, Chase."

"Ditto."

"So you are not backing out?"

Chase stood and stepped toward her. "Oh, no, sweetheart. I never back out of anything. But I do have a proposition for you." He thought about the Christmas in July flyer in his back pocket.

Her brow arched. "Oh?"

Chase inched closer. Wow, in this light, her hazel eyes looked more green than brown. Shaking off that distraction, he peered into those greenish orbs. "Competition."

"What?"

"We can't control which company the town council picks, so let's do this. The Christmas in July festivities start tomorrow downtown. Seems there are some contests. Cookie Decorating. Reindeer Games. Caroling Karaoke. I'm betting I can win more of them than you."

Suddenly, it seemed Sylvia got a little pep in her step. "You forget. I'm a Garland girl. Homegrown and homespun with the hometown advantage."

"I know, and I'm up for it."

"Seriously, Chase. You'll lose."

"And if I do, I'll back out." He sure hoped he had the authority to do that. Bea would have a fit. But he didn't plan on losing, so Bea would never know. Right?

"Really?"

He crossed his heart. "And hope to die."

"Stick a needle in your eye?"

"I won't go that far."

Sylvia smiled. "You're on, Mr. Ellis. Get a good night's sleep. You're going to need it."

I don't intend to lose, Ms. Moore.

Sylvia turned and sashayed up the dock. Chase had to admit, he was somewhat enamored of that sassy sashay.

CHAPTER THREE

Sylvia stalked away from the gazebo and into the inn. Once in the lobby, she noticed a stack of flyers for the week's festivities on a side table. She snatched one and stomped up the stairs to her room.

Her cheeks were flaming hot. Why had she let that man get under her skin? Besides, there was no way she was going to lose a single game to Chase Ellis. This was her town, and those games were hers to win. She wasn't about to forget there was a lot riding on them, more than just bragging rights. She needed this contract to pan out. If it did, this could lead to bigger movie budgets, maybe even international.

She studied the flyer and was confident she could win Caroling Karaoke and Cookie Decorating and she her favorite, Snowmen in July. It took a certain finesse to build a snowman from Styrofoam and not those little craft store versions. She'd bet Chase wouldn't know they came in sizes up to thirty inches. A self-satisfied smile played over her lips as she nodded; she had that event in the bag.

As she continued to plot her strategy, her cell phone buzzed with an incoming text. Her heart sank, and instead of returning the message, she dialed.

Without exchanging pleasantries, she asked, "Aunt Melanie, I got your text. What's this about Uncle Chet's meeting at town hall?"

"Sylvia, your uncle just got home from a meeting, and the town is reviewing your proposal along with that other man's. Chase something or other. Well, anyway, he got his paperwork in before you, and they're seriously considering his. I told your uncle that he needs to stand up and tell them they have to give you the permits; you're one of us."

That took the wind out of her sails. "Aunt Melanie, I just have to get those permits. I basically promised a producer it was a slam dunk." She inwardly groaned, hating when she used sports metaphors to explain herself. But her aunt's love of basketball would add extra punch to the situation.

"I know, Sylvia, and I told Chet that, but he's saying the rules are the rules and his hands are tied."

"I turned my application in today." She smacked her forehead and remembered Chase pulling out that envelope from his pocket while she wrote her letter. She missed getting ahead of him by less than thirty minutes. Surely the council would take that into consideration. "Thanks for letting me know, but I'm not giving up. When I want something badly enough, I can make it happen."

"Alright, Sylvia, let me know if there's anything we can do to help." Her aunt said her goodbyes after reminding her to come by for dinner while she was in town.

She flopped back on her bed, arms flung out to her sides, her thoughts racing. The only way to be sure she had permits in hand by this time next week was to be the big winner at the festival.

The next morning, Sylvia was ready to take on any challenge

to have the film crew arriving in the fall. Determined didn't even begin to describe how she felt.

After getting a coffee and muffin from the breakfast bar, she quickly left the inn. The last person she wanted to run into was… Chase Ellis.

She whipped around, frantically looking for a different path to her car, but before she could disappear, he called to her.

"'Morning, Sylvia."

Gritting her teeth, she forced a smile. "Hey, Chase. I didn't expect to see you up and out so early."

He tipped his head and gave her a slow, sexy grin that made his brown eyes like tempered chocolate, which of course caused her blood to run just a bit warmer. And damn, he looked good in the body-skimming light-blue tee and cargo shorts. She turned away so he wouldn't think she was gawking and get any ideas.

"I'd love to know what's going on in your pretty head. You're blushing."

Great, if he could read her mind, he would definitely get the wrong idea. She fanned a hand in front of her face. "Just warm out this morning."

Nodding, he smirked. "If you say so."

She pointed to the parking area. "Sorry. I gotta get going, but I'll see you later? The first event is cookie decorating at two in the town square."

"Don't worry, sweetheart, I won't be late."

With a shake of her head, she wanted to remind him she was not his sweetheart but chose to ignore him instead. "Catch ya later." Sylvia decided to run by The Evergreen to see if she could get any dirt on Chase from Krissy. It seemed only fair that two could play that game.

When Sylvia strolled into the diner, she inhaled the sweet and spicy scent of cinnamon rolls. She fluttered her fingers in Krissy's direction and took a seat at a small table near the front window. The shop was buzzing with people placing orders to go, and she wasn't in a rush. She noticed the self-serve coffee station. Just what she needed. Time for an extra-large cup before giving her friend a head bob in the direction of the table.

Krissy was finally able to join her about half an hour later. "Sylvia, it's great to see you this morning. How's your trip been?" She leaned in. "Did you get the permit for filming?"

Sylvia glanced out the window and then gave her a long look. "Not exactly. It seems there's a little competition. Do you know anything about what Chase Ellis has been doing that could help me?"

Her friend looked around before saying, "I know he's been talking to folks, getting to know people, and ingratiating himself with the locals, but that was before you got back. I'll bet people will want to support you."

Frowning, Sylvia said, "Well, we kind of have a bet based on who gets the permits. Whoever wins the most events at the festival this week is the winner."

Slapping her hand on the tabletop, she grimaced and her shoulders sagged. As she was saying it out loud, Sylvia knew it was a dumb idea.

"Why on earth would you make a bet like that?"

"I've played all these games for years, and I figured I had the edge." If her shoulders could have sagged any lower, they'd still be dropping.

Krissy sat up a little straighter. "Don't look now, but guess who just walked by."

Sylvia saw him walk in the door. Wasn't the best defense a good offense? Under her breath, she said to Krissy. "Watch this."

She held up her hand. "Chase. Hey."

He quirked an eyebrow and sauntered over. "Fancy meeting you here." He gave Krissy a wide smile. "Are those cinnamon rolls I smell?"

She grinned. "Fresh from the oven. Can I interest you in one?"

He held up two fingers. "We'll each have one, that's if Sylvia will allow me to join her."

She gestured to the now vacant chair since Krissy had jumped up. "Help yourself."

How should she play this? And she was curious which movie he was working on.

He asked, "I'm going to get coffee. Want a refill?"

Now he was being overly nice, but she'd play along. "Thanks." She handed him her cup and watched as he crossed the room and was back within minutes.

He stepped over the seat and straddled the small bistro-style chair. "I must say I'm surprised you asked me to join you."

"The thought crossed my mind that you might follow me and, to be fair, I didn't really invite you. Krissy gave up her chair, and it's the polite thing to do."

He seemed to take what he could get. "Tell me, which is your best event for the week?"

Leaning back in her chair, she was suspicious. Why did he want to know? So he could practice? "Pretty much all of them."

With a snort, he grinned. "Pride does come before the fall."

"Confidence is the key, my friend."

"Ah, so now we're friends?" He sipped his coffee and then added a splash of cream from the small pitcher on the table.

"Don't get carried away; it's just an expression."

His eyes sparkled with laughter, and even as she tried to keep her face expressionless, he had a certain amount of charm just oozing. Where the heck was Krissy with those rolls? If he was eating, he couldn't be trying to chat her up.

"Tell me, did you have a festival like this growing up in Denver?"

"You know I grew up in Colorado? Interesting. Have you been checking me out?"

The smirk on his face also laced his words. Why did he irk her so much? "It always pays to know who I'm up against."

"Nah, I've never been to a festival like what we're about to get tangled up in."

His gaze started at her eyes, then rested on her lips, and she had a powerful urge to lean in and kiss his full mouth. She stammered. "Good, um, good to know."

"But don't go easy on me. I can hold my own in any sort of game."

Why did she get the impression they weren't talking about festival games but something much more interesting? And how did he do this? Keep this banter going with double entendres flying.

"Not to worry."

He pushed back his chair. "I'm going to head out, but you have a good rest of your morning, and sweetheart, I'll see you this afternoon." He tossed a twenty on the table and flashed her what she had discovered was his normal cocky grin.

"What about your cinnamon roll?"

"Tell Krissy I'll pick it up before she closes."

It really grated on her the way he tossed out sweetheart in every conversation they had. But every time she said something, it just seemed to egg him on, so it was better to let it go.

Krissy came over with two small plates after Chase left. "Is he coming back?"

"Chase said he'd be back later, so you might as well box it up." She held out her hand for one of the plates. "But I can't wait to enjoy this sweet treat."

"What's going on between you two, Syl? The air was just about crackling over here with a pending electrical storm."

"It's all about the filming permit, but he just admitted he's never been to a festival like this, so I've got it in the bag." She hoped her voice sounded more confident than she felt. "I can't lose."

Shortly after one o'clock, Sylvia parked her car behind the church and walked across the street to the town square. First up was cookie decorating. Chase was standing near a table, and he smiled the moment he saw her and pointed to a vacant spot next to him. What the heck, she could stand being next to him. At least this way she could see how bad he was doing, and it would bolster her confidence.

"Chase."

"Sylvia. Ready to get your hands on some cookies?"

At each decorating station, there were a dozen sugar cookies, icing, decorating tips, and all kinds of colored sugars and jimmies. Remembering all the years she and her mom decorated cookies, her confidence soared. "Are you ready to suffer your first of many losses?"

He gave her a light shoulder bump. "Oh, darlin', the word *lose* is not in my vocabulary."

CHAPTER FOUR

"Well, bring it on then, dude."

Chase grinned and watched Sylvia's next movements. She set a canvas bag on the table, simultaneously flashing him a sweet smile. From the bag, she pulled out ribbon after ribbon. You know, the kind of ribbons one gets when winning an event, like best pie at the county fair or first place in a horse jumping competition. Some of them boasted big ribbon blossoms at the top, and all sported the words "First Place." Some were red and others blue, but they all signified winners.

"Whatcha got there, Sylvia?" He was curious, to say the least. What was her game?

"Oh, nothing." She rounded the table and began pinning her winning ribbons to the table—front and center—for all to see. "Just a few reminders for the judges and the townsfolk." She spoke while paying attention to her work. "Let's see. This one was for cookie decorating in 2005. I was a teenager. I think my fancy swirls won them over that year. Then this one!" She held up a large blue ribbon. "This one was for my exquisite piping skills. Those cookies were fabulous. I was home from college that summer." She paused, looking over her collection and rifling through them. "But who could forget this gem? My first. I was six, I believe. Most creative use of sprinkles." She smiled at the ribbon with affection and pinned it to the tablecloth.

With a sigh, she finished pinning the rest of the ribbons, brushed her hands together, and lifted her gaze to meet Chase's—again, sporting that sweet, but almost gloating smile. "Intimidated yet?"

Not *almost* gloating. That was a definite gloat she just shot his way.

Chase ambled around his station, rubbed his chin, and contemplated the cheeky Sylvia and her tactics. He had to give her credit. He stared at the ribbons for a long moment, then finally said, "Hmm. Impressive."

"But are you intimidated?"

"Not in the least."

"But why not? You'll be hard-pressed to beat me in this, our opening contest, Mr. Ellis."

He shrugged, then faced Sylvia, looking her square in her sexy hazel orbs. "All talk, no action." He turned and then walked away.

"What the heck does that mean?" she called out.

"Smoke and mirrors, Sylvia. Or should I say, ribbons and rhetoric. Doesn't matter. There's a new guy in town, Ms. Moore, and he's not intimidated by fluff."

"Fluff? Well, I never."

At that point, a loudspeaker crackled. Chase looked at the podium where Krissy stood. He turned his attention her way, but out of the corner of his eye, saw Sylvia round the table. When something square flashed to his left, he watched as she set up a cardboard partition between the two stations. Presumably, so he couldn't see what she was doing.

He turned. "Really?"

"Pay attention to your own station, Mr. Ellis."

"I fully intend to, Ms. Moore."

"Everyone! Everyone!" Krissy called out through the bullhorn. "Attention, please."

Chase turned to look at Krissy but kept his peripheral vision peeled for any movement from his left. Sylvia was hell-bent on winning this thing, and at any cost, apparently. He needed to be on his toes.

Don't count your chickens before they hatch, sweetheart.

"We are about to get started, so please move to your stations!" Krissy paused for a moment, looking about, then continued. "I'm so excited that The Evergreen Diner is sponsoring this year's cookie competition. Such a fine lot of decorators I see out there! Thank you for entering. Your entry fees will go toward the community center fund. I also want to add that the judges for today's contest—as is tradition—are secret. So, decorators? Anyone who stops by your table to watch you decorate or view your finished product could be a judge. Act accordingly! Remember, the rules are simple—you can only use the items on your table. We've provided everything for you. The cookies, especially, so taste-testing is not part of the competition, only how you choose to decorate them. No work ahead of time except for organizing your area. Remember, everyone has thirty minutes to decorate and we will start in ten minutes. Make your final preparations now!"

With that, Chase looked down at his table. He had no idea what half of the decorating paraphernalia was for, but he assumed he could figure it out. Looking left, he leaned slightly to peek over Sylvia's partition. She had her supplies all laid out in some sort of order.

"Look now," she said, fiddling with a couple of bottles of sprinkles, "because in a few minutes you are going to be too busy to pay attention to what I'm doing. Focus on your own self, Chase."

"I fully intend to do just that, Sylvia."

"Good."

"Great."

"Best of luck to you."

"And to you too, sweetheart."

Sylva lifted her gaze, gave him a brief glare, and stuck out her tongue.

"Decorators! Are you ready? Countdown to cookies. Ten, nine, eight, seven..."

The crowd joined in the chant.

Sylvia glared at him with a devilish smile.

Intimidated? Him? No freakin' way.

Chase wished Sylvia had kept her tongue in her mouth. Sticking it out was not only childish, but... Well, distracting.

He didn't have time to contemplate Sylvia's tongue. Not really, and not right now. The competition had started. And all he could do was stand there staring at a dozen sugar cookies and multiple utensils that he had no clue what to do with. He also had no inkling of how to handle the not-so-subtle testosterone-related urges that were sneaking up into his lower gut.

Down, boy. Not now. No time for that.

He had to get moving on those cookies. His business all but depended on landing the permits for this movie. Bea would have his tail in a sling if he lost out, and the thing with Bea was that she talked. A lot. To others in the business.

Then get busy with the cookies, Ellis!

But the image of Sylvia's tongue darting between her pink lips intrigued him. Her tongue had lingered in that position for a split second and then casually raked over her lower lip before descending back into her pouty mouth.

That's what stayed with him. The tip of her tongue between her two lips.

Gah. Forget it!

The image flustered him and held his attention the entire

twenty minutes he attempted to decorate boring round cookies into some sort of Christmas confection perfection.

It wasn't happening.

But he got to work, anyway. How difficult could it be? Not willing to risk looking over the partition to his left, he sidled a speedy glance to the cookie decorator on his right. Hmm. He promptly assessed. She used the frosting as a base on the cookie, the confections on top. She picked up a bag full of… was that frosting? …and swirled it around the edges.

He could do that. Surely. Right?

"Looks like you're off to a slow start, Chase. Everything okay?"

Startled, he dragged his gaze back to his station and looked up. Krissy stood there, eyeballing his undecorated contest entries.

He arched a brow. "Are you cavorting with the enemy?"

Krissy's brows scrunched. "What?"

He ticked his head to the left. "Ms. Cookie Decorator Winner send you over here to check out my technique? Because I assure you, Ms. Krissy, my technique is unique." That didn't come out right.

Krissy laughed. "I'm sure it is. When do I get to see it?"

Chase picked up a bag of icing. "I'm working on it. Later. Be gone with you." He waved her away, bag of frosting in hand.

A voice came from his left, on the other side of the partition. "Then you better get crackin', mister. You have twenty-seven minutes."

"Oh! That's right. I must remind people of the time soon." Krissy lifted the bullhorn to her mouth and hurried off toward the podium. After a couple of minutes, she shouted out, "Twenty-five minutes remaining, decorators!"

Chase inwardly groaned. He shot a look at Sylvia. She beamed at him over the cardboard and then went back to work.

Let's see. A dozen cookies. Twenty-five minutes. He could spend two minutes per cookie with seconds to spare.

He picked up a long spatula, dipped it into the frosting, and slathered it on a cookie.

The decorator on his right leaned his way. "Brush the crumbs off first for a smoother effect."

He stared at the woman. "Thanks."

Everyone's an expert. Or a critic. Or both.

He blocked them all out. Right. Left. And in front of him. He had work to do. A contest to win. A permit to secure. A client to please.

So. Much. On. The. Line.

"Time's up! Spatulas down. Step away from your stations, decorators."

Chase did just that. Wiping his hands on a paper towel, he stared at his plated cookies, feeling proud of himself. He'd done a half-decent job if he said so himself. Actually, he did an excellent job, given the circumstances and his relative lack of experience.

But hey, what he lacked in experience he made up for with heart, soul, and motivation. Right?

Krissy picked up the bullhorn again. "Can I have all the decorators up front, please?" She waved toward the podium. "Leave your cookies at your stations. The judges want to take one last stroll through the entries. That's right, up this way. Thank you! Just gather over there..." She pointed and people started lining up.

Chase rounded his station while Sylvia removed the cardboard partition. Only then did he get a full gander at her confections. His heart sank. The woman was indeed amazing. Her swirls and dips and doodles and sprinkles and... Why, she even had faces on some cookies and a stocking painted on another and… Good God almighty, had she painted an entire nativity scene on that one?

"Intimidated yet?" The goading came from behind his left shoulder. He didn't have to turn to know whose voice.

He shrugged. "You've got skills, baby, that's a given. But my cookies? They have heart. And character. I'm sure the judges will notice that." He headed for the podium.

Sylvia caught up with him, giggling. "What a crock of baloney."

He wanted to smile. He didn't. "Oh? You don't believe in heart, Sylvia?"

"This contest is won on skill, Chase. There are no prizes here for participation or consolation or… character."

"We will see about that."

"Yes, we will."

Krissy shouted into the bullhorn again. "Decorators! We are ready to announce the winner! Gather 'round, everyone."

They fell into the decorator crowd and waited.

Sylvia leaned in. "Sorry about your loss."

Chase stood solidly beside her, watching Krissy talk with the judges. "Sorry about your ego. I'll be walking away with this one."

Shaking her head, Sylvia bumped his arm. "Not in this life."

"Remains to be seen. Oh, look. Krissy has the judges' decision."

"Get ready to eat crow, Ellis."

"No crow for me, darlin', but I was thinking about lasagna at that Italian restaurant by the lake later. Join me?" He turned to look at her then and almost laughed at her facial expression.

"What?" She stared, her eyes as round as saucers. "Excuse me?"

The bullhorn crackled. "We have a winner! Drumroll,

please. This year's cookie decorating contest winner is…" Krissy drew out the last words.

Sylvia dragged her gaze away from Chase to look at Krissy. "Come on, Kris. Get this over with. Say my name!"

"Better yet, say mine," Chase murmured.

"The winner is… Melissa Hampton! I believe this is her first win. Congrats, Melissa!"

Chase stood stone-still, watching Krissy and the winner. He had no words. A myriad of thoughts raced through his head. Finally, he shifted to look at Sylvia, who also stood staring straight ahead, biting her lip.

Neither of them won. He'd never considered outsiders. He had to up his game.

CHAPTER FIVE

How could she have lost the cookie decorating competition? Dazed, Sylvia wanted to stomp over to Krissy and demand to know why she hadn't announced Sylvia as the winner. Her friend knew everything was riding on those filming permits. Friends were supposed to have each other's backs. That's the way this was supposed to work.

"Well, that was a kick in the butt." Chase nodded in Krissy's direction. "No one can accuse her of bias."

The frown slipped from one side of her face to the other, and she didn't care. "True, but I wasn't prepared to lose."

His eyes never left her face. "Have you given any thought to what happens if neither of us wins any of the events? After all, we should consider the possibility. There are other people entering these competitions."

As if he needed to point out they might be on the losing end of the week. "Maybe you should withdraw your permit application now and leave Garland to me."

His eyes narrowed, and the genuine concern that had been on his face faded and turned to stone. "Not about to happen, sweetheart. All's fair in love and business."

With a slow, unbelieving shake of her head and a snort,

Sylvia walked away from the group of decorators to pick up her supplies and wipe down the table. All she wanted to do was get away from here.

"Where are you going?"

She glanced over her shoulder and discovered Chase was trailing behind her. She missed the smile that usually graced his oh so kissable mouth. Where had that thought come from? She pulled her gaze away from his handsome face, reminding herself she didn't need to get caught up in anything other than winning those stupid permits.

"Outta here." Under her breath, she muttered, "Not that you care."

"Darlin', that's not fair."

He was so close she could smell his woodsy cologne and the sweet scent of frosting. Both caused her stomach to flip with a stab of longing she was trying hard to ignore. She noticed a small streak of icing on his cheek, and her fingers itched, wanting to reach out and wipe it off. Heck, she could think of another way to get it off.

She muttered, "Focus."

Chase furrowed his brow. "Excuse me? What exactly am I supposed to focus on?"

She wanted to sink through the gazebo floor. Had she said that out loud? It's not like she could tell him about her ideas of frosting. Heat flushed her cheeks as she did her best to keep her breathing even.

With a poke of her finger in his direction, she said, "I need to focus on the next event. Caroling Karaoke. You should think about what song you're going to choose."

He stuck his hands in the front pockets of his cargo shorts. "Have dinner with me, and we can talk about the next challenge. Maybe we shouldn't be so focused on beating each other and remember there's other competition. We could join forces, you know."

He had a point. She had never considered that other

people might be competing. In her mind, she had pushed away the possibility that there were other people who could win; it had been just about the two of them. "You mean like we didn't do today? I underestimated this event, but I won't do that again."

She looked away, and as much as she wanted to say yes to dinner, the words that came out of her mouth were the only ones she could articulate. "I'm not sure dinner is a good idea. Discussing how we can join forces won't put either of us in a position to beat the other, and that's what this is all about. The filming permits."

Chase touched her arm, but she kept her face averted so he wouldn't be able to see her eyes. On many occasions, she'd been told that she was a terrible liar, and having dinner with the man standing behind her, who made her pulse race, was something she wanted to do. Lingering over a glass of ruby red chianti and Italian was her idea of an ideal date. Under different circumstances, she'd say yes, maybe, but not now.

"Suit yourself. But if you change your mind, I'll be at Luigi's around six."

Sylvia didn't turn, but heard his fading footsteps. All she had wanted to do was say yes. What would it hurt to have dinner with a good-looking man? It didn't negate the competition and she was still determined to get the permits at all costs. Her business was riding on her success.

Her cell rang, and she pulled it from her back pocket. Inwardly, she groaned. "This is Sylvia."

It was easier to pretend she didn't know who was on the other end and sound professional.

"Sylvia, it's Jessica. I was checking to see if you have some dates for when the advance film crew should plan on arriving in town. We have a two-week production schedule to get the movie filmed and into postproduction, and if you can deliver, I have a few more projects lined up that are in your wheelhouse."

A flicker of hope for her future was overshadowed by what she was about to say. "There's been a minor delay. I'm, um, waiting for the selection board to meet, and there's a festival going on so the town is a bit focused on fun and not business." She crossed her fingers like she had when she was a kid, hoping to keep bad karma away from her fib.

A loud sigh reached her ears, and Sylvia could picture Jessica tapping her short, manicured nails on her glass-topped desk. "Alright, well, keep me informed of your progress and as soon as it's a lock, let me know. We have everyone on standby, waiting to make final plans."

"You got it."

"And Sylvia, remember I'm counting on you to bring this to a close and soon."

She heard the unmistakable warning tone in Jessica's voice. "I won't let you down." The sound of the line being disconnected was actually music to her ears. She didn't want to continue the conversation any longer to keep the lies from growing.

Later in the day, Sylvia struck out for a walk around Sullivan's Pond. She needed to clear her head and try to come up with a plan to sweep the next two events, the Caroling Karaoke and the Build a Snowman contest. But she couldn't think of a way to ensure she'd beat anyone, let alone Chase. Even if they both lost, they weren't any closer to deciding who was going to get the permits. She dropped to a weathered wooden bench and tipped her head back, savoring the feel of the warm sun against her skin. She had forgotten the simple pleasure of being in the moment and in Garland. She looked around, knowing this would be a good place to film if only the pond was frozen over, but that wouldn't be the case in the fall. She'd have to set a shoot at the hockey rink and pray it would work.

But now she looked at the area with fresh eyes. This was perfect for another upcoming project that she was vying for. But would it matter if she failed to secure Garland? Jessica was very difficult, and she could put the word out that Sylvia couldn't deliver the locations, and it would cause irreparable damage to her career. Even if there were other locations, Garland was perfect.

She tapped her chin with her finger. *"What if I help Chase scout for a new location? Maybe he'd walk away from Garland. There are other towns nearby with a similar vibe."* Pleased with herself, she got up from the bench. It was time to do some research, then put on a sundress and a touch of makeup. It never hurt to look good, but not like she was trying too hard either. She'd show up for dinner, or at least they could have a drink together as respected rivals, and she'd present the new options to him. With that problem nearly solved, all that was left was to make a list of surrounding towns; after all, this was New England, and quaint small towns were plentiful.

With a lighter outlook, she strolled back to her car and made a quick stop at the Chamber of Commerce to pick up some brochures. They should have a few pamphlets from the neighboring towns and what they had to offer.

After she finished at the Chamber, she drove past the town hall and noticed Chase taking the front steps two at a time. She slowed the car, and the itch to follow him was almost overwhelming. What was he up to now? Her plan made more sense, and it would give him a reason to leave town. Resisting the urge to go after him, she turned her thoughts to the task she had to get done—outline her proposition and be prepared to pitch it, showing him the options in the best light possible.

At six o'clock, Sylvia sat at the bar, her eyes on the door while she toyed with a glass of red wine. She had dressed carefully to highlight her eyes and figure, opting for a lavender A-line sundress, high-heeled strappy sandals, and her long hair pulled back from her face. Sitting on the bar was a folder she had prepared for Chase. It was a long shot, but she still hoped he'd agree to withdraw his submission to the town. She glanced at her phone to check the time. Six fifteen. He hadn't arrived yet, and she wondered if he'd changed his mind. She waited a little longer since he had mentioned arriving around six. Almost six thirty, the door opened, and he stepped inside, pausing as his gaze swept the interior. His smile widened when he saw her perched on a stool at the bar. Sylvia raised her glass, trying to act nonchalant while acknowledging his presence. Her heartbeat quickened as he approached her, and her mouth went dry, like the Mojave Desert. He might be competition, but the way he made her body tingle was totally unexpected and oh so nice.

CHAPTER SIX

Chase grinned, attempting to hide his delight in seeing Sylvia seated at the bar, but paused for a moment before stepping farther into the restaurant. He'd figured no way in hell would she join him for dinner. But there she was, looking like summer on a fancy dessert plate, holding up that sparkling glass of wine and nodding to him with a cute—and dare he think?—come-hither smile on her face.

His heart jackknifed.

He'd always been drawn to her. They'd shared a mutual back-and-forth, teasing banter, on more than one occasion when meeting at business-related events. Several times they'd been in similar positions—both vying for a shoot location. But then, things hadn't heated up between them like what was happening now.

Something was different. What was it?

He'd pondered that earlier in the day, too, after the cookie competition. He'd known what was happening on his side of things—he was extremely eager to land this particular site to please a major client who could promise more work for his growing business. This was a critical land for him. But what was her game? Why was she so intent on winning this location out from under him?

Something was at stake for her, too. Was it more than her growing up here? That she still had family and friends in Garland?

Maybe.

He sauntered her way, weaving through a small crowd of people, and headed for the empty seat next to hers at the bar. With each step, his heart kicked up its tempo and his breathing grew shallow. She looked beautiful sitting there—perhaps prettier than he'd ever seen her, or maybe had noticed—waiting for him. And if he were truly honest with himself, he liked the notion of her waiting for him, like they were a couple or something.

He halted in his tracks.

Whoa! Is that it?

The thing that was different now?

Ambling toward her, he focused the direction of his thoughts. He was more than drawn to her—he was full-blown attracted to her romantically. He'd waved the attraction off in the past. Their banter and camaraderie were just fun. But now, it was like her body was physically and emotionally tugging him toward her on a string connecting their two hearts. As he approached the empty bar seat, he blew out a shaking breath and looked deep into her hazel eyes.

Or were they green? Gold? With a hint of lavender? All the above. Yes, hazel.

A magical sort of twinkle reflected in those eyes as he eased into the seat. Her complexion was dewy and flawless. Her cheeks glowed. And every fiber of his being wanted to scoot his bar chair as close as possible and nuzzle into her soft neck and silky auburn tresses, and—

"I decided to join you after all, Chase. I hope you don't mind."

He pulled back slightly and blinked, righting his brain. Somewhat. Now he knew what was different. It wasn't the competition or the rivalry. There was some sort of magnetic, mysterious, and wonderful connection between them that wasn't there before. One that made him want to kiss her, right there on the spot.

Which, of course, he wouldn't. Not yet. And not here.

"Chase?"

"Oh. Sylvia. No, I don't mind. I…" He paused, playing his gaze over her features again. "I'm happy you're here." *Very happy*. He'd never noticed the smattering of freckles on her nose before. They were very faint, but cute, and they gave her face character. He'd like to kiss them.

One. By. One.

He was putty in her hands. She held him spellbound.

Chase shook himself. *Get a grip, man*. "I'd hoped you'd change your mind."

Sylvia nodded. "Yes. I thought about it. Thought about a lot of things this afternoon, actually. One I'd like to talk to you about."

"Oh?" There was something he'd like to talk to her about, too. Like what color of lip gloss she wore on those kissable, blushingly pink lips of hers. And perhaps, discuss how she was feeling about him, too. Was she just as smitten with him? Did they share a mutual magnetism?

"Yes. I was thinking—"

"Sir, your table is ready." Interrupted by the restaurant host, Chase pivoted as the gentleman stepped closer to the couple. "I have a quiet table for you, as requested. This way, please." He swept his arm to his left.

Chased stood and nodded toward Sylvia, reaching for her arm. "Let's continue this discussion in a minute. Shall we?"

Sylvia gracefully rose from the chair, giving him another captivating smile. He watched as she tucked a folder into her bag, then reached for her wineglass. He wondered, briefly, what was in that folder, but dismissed that curiosity as he settled his hand at the small of her back. They crossed the room, following the host to a cozy and secluded table for two in the corner.

Perfect.

With Sylvia's approval, Chase ordered an appetizer of calamari to start with. The server brought Sylvia more wine and Chase an old-fashioned. They maintained a few moments of idle chitchat, then ordered. Sylvia requested a side salad and shrimp scampi. Chase suddenly felt ravenous and went for the lasagna with a meaty antipasto salad on the side.

Their salads came and the small talk continued. Chase was content to sit, chat, and look at Sylvia over his salad. In no time, it seemed the server had whisked their salad dishes away and placed the entrees in front of them.

"That's quite some dinner there, Chase," Sylvia said several minutes later. "I wondered how you would put away all that antipasto, and now that your lasagna is here, I'm amazed you can eat a bite."

Chase chuckled. "Growing boy here." He glanced out the window, thinking. "You know, I think I skipped lunch. After taking care of some business this morning, I went straight to the cookie contest." He looked at her, catching her gaze again. A flicker of candlelight reflected in her eyes, which now looked dark green. The low light, however, made her overall look soft and sultry and… yes, sexy. He inhaled, exhaled, calmed his libido. A little. "Suddenly, I'm ravenous."

Am I talking about lasagna, or her?

Never mind, Ellis. Focus.

"Well, that was an intense competition," Sylvia said. "We probably both worked up an appetite. I'm still shocked that one of us didn't win. You did make a halfway decent effort,

Chase, but there is no denying my cookies were superior." She paused, toying with the shrimp on her plate with her fork. "I still can't believe Kris let that happen, that the judges picked Melissa Hampton to win. Did you see her cookies? Nothing original there."

Chase chewed a bit of gooey lasagna, then raised an eyebrow. "Are you saying Krissy should have intervened in the judges' decision?"

"Oh, no." Sylvia shook her head and set down her fork. "Not at all. I know it would not be fair of her to do that. Even if she is my best friend. But it's just disappointing because…" Her words drifted off.

Chase laid his fork down too and watched her stare at the tablecloth. "Because?"

Slowly, Sylvia lifted her gaze and connected with his. "Chase, I'm going to level with you."

He leaned forward. "Please do, Sylvia."

"I need to land this location."

"As do I."

She nodded. "I know. I'm sure you have your reasons. I have mine too." She stared into his eyes and reached across the table. Her hand lay there, palm up, as if she were expecting him to lay his hand in hers. He hesitated, then slowly did.

He exhaled deeply as their skin touched. Her palm was warm, soft. Her touch an invitation? How long had he been holding that breath? Forever?

"Sylvia…"

She interrupted. "I wouldn't ask this of you, Chase, if it weren't important. My reputation and business are on the line. I'm in danger of losing it all if I don't nail the permits to film in Garland. Look, I know this area well, and I've done my research. There are other small towns that should suffice for you. Like Charmington, where we are staying at the Holly Hill Inn. And Grace Cove, Noel, and Maple Falls. And I will help you find another location if you will kindly back out of this one."

Well, that was unexpected. Chase pulled his hand away.

"In fact." Sylvia reached to the floor where her purse sat. He watched her retrieve the mystery folder and lay it on the table. "I worked on this after the cookie competition. I don't think our bet on the events is going to work. We didn't consider that other people could win and upset our applecart. So, I've prepared a strategy to help you land another town. Based on my research, Grace Cove would be perfect. My number one pick. Charmington comes a close second. And Maple Falls is absolutely charming. These are all excellent choices. Please pull out of the running here in Garland. I would be eternally grateful."

Chase stared at the folder. He could consider her offer, or he could stomp off in anger that she'd even suggested it. He sat back in his chair. "I'll take a look and think about it."

"There's not much time. The town council meets in one day."

He knew that. He fingered the edge of the folder and flipped back the cover. Her so-called strategy was outlined crisp and clean on the front-page overview. She'd obviously done her homework.

His gaze lifted. "I don't understand why you would do this."

"I need Garland, Chase. I know you need it too. But I will help you find another town."

"I'm clearly in the lead here, according to the people I've talked to downtown. Why would I do that?"

Sylvia bit her lip, then smiled hesitantly. "For me? Please?"

Oh, don't go there.

She batted her eyes and leaned into the table. Her sundress gaped a little, showing a bit of cleavage. Did she realize that?

My God. Was she using him? Pretending there was an attraction? Just to get her way?

No. Not happening. He stood and snatched up the folder. Even if he had no intention to do her bidding, he wanted to see what she had to offer. "I'm suddenly not hungry. You're right. That antipasto filled me up. Please stay and finish your dinner. I'll take this,"—he held up the folder—"back to the inn. I'll let you know something tomorrow."

She looked up and met his stare. "I was hoping to get your answer tonight."

Chase pulled his wallet out of his pocket and placed several bills on the table. "This should be enough to cover dinner. Enjoy."

He was shaking inside, suddenly angry—but even more, confused and disappointed—and just wanted away from the table and the restaurant and frankly, her, for a moment. He needed air and space. How had he been duped into thinking there was some sort of magical attraction between them? She was obviously putting out those signals just to get her way.

"Chase, wait."

He turned and wove his way through the tables. He might have heard heels clicking behind him, but he didn't turn to find out. Pushing through the restaurant door, he strode across the parking lot toward his vehicle.

"Chase, wait! Please."

When he reached his rental car, he turned and faced her. Sylvia must have been coming up fast because when he did, she stumbled and bumped into him hard, their bodies crammed up against each other. Chase leaned back into the car and grasped her around the waist, righting her.

"Crap. My sandal broke!" Reaching down, she examined her shoe.

"Are you okay?"

"I think so. Damn shoe. The strap pulled out. They were new, too."

"Sorry about that."

"It's okay. Not your fault."

At those words, Sylvia finally stopped fidgeting and gradually looked up and into his eyes. Unexpectedly, all his anger whooshed away and something else replaced it.

Desire? Passion? Curiosity?

His hands moved from her waist to her face, cupping her cheeks with his palms. Her gaze didn't falter, and her body leaned in closer. The pleasure of her body aligning with his took him abruptly off-kilter and involuntarily, he gently pulled her tighter into him, their mouths a breath apart.

"This is not a good idea," Sylvia whispered.

"No. No, it's not."

Her chest rose and plunged, the pace of her breathing intensifying. His entire upper body felt taut, like a spring wound too tight inside that was about to burst.

Her breath fanned over his mouth.

"Chase..."

"Sylvia?"

"Kiss me?"

The spring sprung. Chase wove his fingers through her hair and tugged her closer. Their mouths danced over each other's softly for a delicious moment, and then the kiss deepened.

CHAPTER SEVEN

Sylvia took a step closer as Chase wrapped his arms around her, crushing her to his chest as his lips claimed hers. Blood roared in her veins, and she felt alive. The sensations racing through her body were like nothing she had ever experienced before. She clung to him, urging him to deepen the kiss. And then she froze. What was she doing kissing Chase Ellis, the man who could single-handedly destroy her company? She inserted her hand between their bodies and pushed back, looking away, shocked to have let herself get caught up in the moment. Turning on what was left of her broken sandal, she hobbled away.

"Sylvia. Wait!" Now it was his turn to follow her.

The door locks chirped on her rental car, and she slid behind the wheel, turned the engine over, and gunned from the parking space, not caring that her tires squealed. She drove like the devil was chasing her and, in some ways, he was. Tongue-dancing with Chase might be as close to fraternizing with the enemy as she wanted to get.

She glanced in her rearview mirror, confirming he wasn't following her. A part of her heart was heavy with regret. She wished he was. He was like the jelly to her peanut butter, which happened to be her all-time favorite sandwich.

Main Street twinkled with white lights strung for the festival, and in December, they would shine bright again. With a heavy feeling in her gut, she knew in her heart she was the only person who should film the next holiday movie in Garland. Her hands clenched the steering wheel just a little tighter. Why couldn't Chase understand that? Driving slowly past the diner, she looked for a light on in the kitchen, hoping Krissy would be there, but the shop was dark. For a moment she thought of driving over to see her aunt and uncle, but in her present mood she wasn't fit company. With no place left to go, she turned around and headed back to Holly Hill Inn.

Sylvia approached the porch with a broken sandal in hand and the other still on her foot. Her halting steps slowed when she noticed Chase sitting in the shadows drinking a beer. *Kissing him hadn't been the problem; wanting to keep kissing him was.*

"Hey." The single word came out of his mouth as a low, sexy rumble that caused her stomach to flip.

"How long have you been sitting out here?" She didn't bother to ask why. It would be obvious to a wooden post he was waiting for her. They had unfinished business.

With a shoulder shrug, he stated, "A while."

One- and two-word answers weren't going to cut it. She walked closer and gestured to the empty chair next to him. "Mind if I sit?"

He lifted his eyes. Sarcasm dripped as he said, "It's your hometown."

And there it was. "If you are enjoying the evening, I don't want to intrude."

There was a pregnant pause. Finally, he said, "I've been waiting for you."

The slight accusing tone came through loud and clear, as if she had inconvenienced him by not coming straight back to the inn.

"I didn't know I needed to check in with you." Instantly, she regretted the sharpness in her voice, but she sure wouldn't be apologizing.

"You don't, but we have unfinished business." His words echoed her thoughts.

She hoped the darkness covered the heat rising in her cheeks. "Did you look at the papers?"

He turned to face her. "Is that all you ever think about? Business? Or was kissing me part of your plan to coerce me to give up this location?"

Her hand flew to her throat. "No." The word escaped on a breath, shocked that he could think she would stoop that low. But why wouldn't he jump to that conclusion? This business was filled with people who used any possible tool to get what they wanted. But how would he know that wasn't her style? They had been skirting each other for several years as casual acquaintances, despite the attraction between them. If she had felt it, he must have as well.

The solar lights blinked on, and she saw he had quirked a brow and tipped his chin down, meeting her eyes in challenge. He didn't believe her. "Why did you kiss me?"

She twisted the strap of her handbag around her wrist. There wasn't any logical way to explain she hadn't thought about the why; she just acted. "Moth to a flame?"

A smile tugged at the corners of his lush, oh so kissable mouth, and once again she wanted to crush herself to his chest and get lost in him.

"Is that your way of saying I'm hot?"

Without looking away, she snapped, "Now you're just being a jerk. I was trying to convey that the moment you got up from the table and stormed out, all thoughts but following you flew out of my head." She gestured to the space between the two of them, then sputtered, "And you know what happened next."

Setting his beer on the side table, he leaned closer but didn't touch her. Dropping his voice to a low, sexy rumble, he asked, "Are you still feeling like the moth?"

Oh, how she wanted to meet him more than halfway, but she needed to stay focused on the real prize, the Garland location. Who was she trying to convince? Chase was quickly dominating her thoughts over anything to do with work.

She shook her head, her mouth too dry to speak and not trusting herself either.

He leaned back and crossed his ankle over the opposite knee, his posture relaxed and that damnable smile still on his face.

"So convince me why I should walk away from the best location I've found for my movie and hand it to you on a Christmas cookie tray."

This was going to be easy. Sylvia knew the surrounding towns almost as well as she knew Garland.

"If you'd just look at my notes, you'll see how all the locations have the same vibe. The only real thing missing is the towns aren't named Garland."

"But this is the only town that celebrates Christmas twice a year."

"True, but they all have town squares, ponds for skating, and lots of holiday activities." With a one-shoulder shrug, she hoped she sounded nonchalant. "If you've seen one small town, you've seen them all, right?"

His eyes widened for a split second and then returned to normal. "If that's the case and they're all alike, why don't you pick one of those towns?"

Chase would never understand how she felt, being the hometown girl and losing the shoot to a guy from Colorado, even if he was smoking hot and made her think about things that had nothing to do with being on Santa's nice list. She toyed with the idea of being up front with him; if she lost, she'd be humiliated. Maybe that was too strong a word, but she'd be embarrassed at the very least.

"You wouldn't understand." She rose to her feet. Her broken sandal in one hand, she slipped the other off her foot. Now barefoot, she felt like a teenager again, hoping the guy would get the hint and kiss her good night before she went into the house.

He stood up and placed his hands on her upper arms, his touch light, but the heat warmed her from head to toes. Why did her body have to react to him like this?

"I do. It would be embarrassing if the select board granted a permit to an interloper, especially when you're vying for the exact same approval. But I followed all the rules, got my paperwork in ahead of yours, and as much as I would love to see you smile at me again and maybe agree to have dinner with me as your date, I won't walk away from this opportunity. I need this, Sylvia, more than you realize."

Was it possible his company would be on the line if he didn't deliver, just as hers was? How could they work around this impasse and enjoy time with each other? Heaven knows she wanted that. Maybe more than she wanted the permits.

Softly, she said, "I need this too."

He dropped his hands from her arms and took a step back. The resignation of the situation hit her hard, and by his downcast eyes, she suspected he felt the same way. Physical attraction aside, she must be a businesswoman first. "Do me one favor. Read the information I've pulled together."

"Okay, but unless something is in there that I might have missed when scouting the county, I won't change my mind."

"Fair enough." She nodded. "Good night, Chase." She stood on tiptoes and brushed her lips over his cheek, lingering close to him, willing him to change his mind about

Garland, and then they could explore this undeniable attraction between them.

He didn't stop her as she walked inside.

The next morning, Sylvia stumbled out of bed and noticed the folder she had given Chase last night had been slipped under her door. As she picked it up, a slip of paper with the inn's logo fluttered to the floor. It was a note from Chase.

Sylvia, much as I wish I could give you what you want, I can't
Maybe you should consider Grace Cove.
I wish things were different.
C-

She flicked the folder onto the bed and dropped into a chair. The only hope she had was if the board ruled in her favor, and with her uncle on the board, he could persuade them. Looking for her cell, she texted her aunt, asking if she could stop over. It wasn't five minutes later that her aunt said the coffee would be hot and fresh. Sylvia couldn't help but think she'd need a gallon to get through today.

On the small table in the screened-in porch, Aunt Melanie had left a carafe of what Sylvia assumed was coffee and a plate covered by a linen napkin and three mugs. Could she have made cinnamon rolls or some other delicious treat, and the extra mug meant her uncle was going to join them? That would work out perfectly.

"There you are." Aunt Melanie came bustling out of the side door with a small tray that held a pitcher, sugar bowl, small plates, and bright-pink napkins. Her aunt loved to serve coffee with a touch of sass. She offered her cheek to Sylvia for a kiss.

"Hi, Auntie. You didn't have to go to all this trouble." She peeked under the napkin-covered plate and saw triple berry muffins. Her mouth watered at the sight and smell.

"Syl, you come to town once in a blue moon, so I wanted to do more than just pour coffee. Besides, this gave me a good excuse to bake." She put a finger over her lips and dropped her voice to a conspiratorial whisper. "The doctor told your uncle he needed to watch his calorie intake."

A stab of worry jabbed at her stomach. "Is he okay?"

"Nothing serious." She glanced over Sylvia's shoulder. "There he is now."

Uncle Chet walked up the steps. It wasn't hard to miss that he moved slower than she remembered. Sylvia needed to get back home more often and vowed she would.

Her uncle gave her a broad smile. "This is a nice surprise." He glanced at his bride of fifty-plus years. "Muffins?"

"I thought Sylvia would like something home-baked since she'll be going back to LA soon."

Uncle Chet gave her a long look and took a chair, then gestured for his wife and niece to join him. "I guess we might as well address the elephant in the room."

Sylvia perched on the edge of a wicker chair and held her breath.

His smile had evaporated. "This time tomorrow the official announcement will be made, but sweetheart, I'm sorry to say the vote was unanimous and the permits are going to Chase Ellis."

CHAPTER EIGHT

Why he felt bad about leaving, Chase wasn't sure, but as he drove away from Holly Hill Inn, a wad of nerves collected deep in his belly and landed with a definitive thump.

He should have faced Sylvia at breakfast and talked with her directly, handing her the folder and telling her the truth. About her proposal. About securing the movie location. And about how he felt about her.

Instead, he'd acted like an awkward adolescent schoolboy, slipped her hard work under her bedroom door with a scribbled note, then turned tail and ran.

Oh, he'd given her proposal a cursory look before going to bed and had flipped through it again before coffee earlier that morning. It didn't take him long to realize it was quality work. Now, he wondered if he'd given it enough serious consideration.

His gut reaction came out of fear, he realized now, which was why he left early. He'd checked out of the inn and figured he'd stay in another town tonight, after he finished his business in Garland today. He had plenty to do. There were a couple of homes in town he wanted to secure for the shoot. He'd already gotten permission to use Holly Hill Inn for some shots, even though it wasn't in Garland, with Kat and Dylan. Maybe that was a backup plan, he wasn't certain. But keeping busy was good. The best thing he could do for himself right now was stay away from Sylvia until the selection announcement tomorrow morning.

He'd check back in with her then, just to make sure all was okay between them.

At least, that was his thinking earlier. Now, he wondered if perhaps he'd knee-jerked his reaction. If he landed the deal like he fully expected, that could be awkward.

He should turn around and go back to the inn. Not avoid her until tomorrow.

Maybe. In a minute. He needed to think a bit more. Driving always helped him think.

Perhaps she was right. There were several small towns in the area that could fit his needs, but Bea had specifically wanted Garland because of its notoriety. Great press down the road, she'd said, when the movie came out, with so many people visiting the town during the December Christmas festival.

He should have considered Sylvia's proposal.

His ego got the better of him.

But that was only part of it. Wasn't it?

The truth was, Sylvia pulled together an excellent proposal in record time. Much better than he would have done—or what he did on a regular basis. If she pulled together as professional a proposal for the Garland town council, as the one she presented to him, he was in trouble.

Therefore, the fear factor. The wavering niggle of doubt in his gut.

The gig might not be in the bag, as he had previously thought.

For the first time this week, he was worried he might not land the shoot. Then what would he do? His boastful nature, his demeanor of confidence, were dwindling. And running away meant he might not get the girl, too.

Did he want the girl? More than the location?

Hell yes, he did.

Chase braked and spun his rented SUV around.

Was he an idiot?

Parked in the middle of the country road, he contemplated the direction of his thoughts. Why had he not realized this before now?

Sylvia was right. Any small town in New England would do for his shoot. He could make any of them work. That was his job, to make sure a setting was exactly what the producer wanted, and he was good at what he did.

Then... Why was he quibbling over something so insignificant?

Why was he not chasing after the girl instead of the town?

Sylvia Moore was not insignificant. He cared for her. He was extremely attracted to her. She could quite possibly, potentially speaking, be the love of his life. He couldn't let that go.

Could he?

No.

And he wasn't about to let something as silly as a tug-of-war over a job get in the way.

Funny thing, as he headed back into Garland, that quavering thud in his stomach dissipated with each mile he put behind him, each mile he was closer to Sylvia. He was doing the right thing.

He was sure of it.

Chase couldn't wait to see the look on her face when he told her the news—that he was backing out and that she'd be the only company vying for the location. It made his heart feel good that he could give this to her. Then, as soon as he told her that news, he'd gather her into his arms and kiss the heck out of her.

Properly, this time.

His heartbeat kicked into a higher gear as he thought about it.

Whether Sylvia would turn out to be the love of his life, he didn't know. But what he knew was that he had to find out. He could not let this opportunity slip through his fingers.

Turning down the main street and into the commons, he parked near the gazebo and sat for a moment, looking off toward the town hall. He hadn't expected to see Sylvia so soon, but there she was, standing in front of the building, stopping a well-dressed woman headed inside. Sylvia's arms flailed about in animation. Chase recognized the other woman from her picture in the town hall lobby. It was Liz Sullivan, the mayor of Garland, who had now planted her feet and was listening with intent to Sylvia's rant.

Pushing open the SUV door, he stepped out onto the pavement, then onto the sidewalk. As he approached Sylvia and the mayor from behind, he noticed another woman determinedly hustling toward Sylvia from the opposite direction. The woman had a bead on Sylvia like a hawk on prey.

She looked a mite out of place—sunglasses, low-cut halter top underneath a short jacket, an equally short flouncy skirt, and three-inch heels. She looked like LA lost in the country.

Shit. Was this Sylvia's boss?

The woman halted beside the pair just a few steps ahead of him, stepping up behind Sylvia, who was still obliviously talking to the mayor.

"Liz, you have to hear me out on this. Can we go inside and talk?"

Mayor Liz Sullivan glanced at her watch. "I'd love to, Sylvia, but I have a full schedule today. Can we do this tomorrow?"

Shaking her head, Sylvia responded. "No. Tomorrow is too late. It's about the permits for the movie shoots later this fall—the one I'm in competition with—"

Chase touched her elbow. "Sylvia, let's talk about that."

She whirled at his touch and glared at him, jerking her elbow away. "What? Oh, Chase. You startled me."

"Sorry. I didn't mean to. Can we talk?" He glanced at the mayor and nodded. "Would you excuse us for a moment?"

"Of course." Liz edged toward the building. He had the feeling she was glad of his interruption.

But Sylvia turned back to Liz, grasping her forearm. "No. Please. I just need a minute." Only then did she seem to spot the other woman standing a few feet away from the mayor. Her eyes flew wide. "Jessica? What are you doing here?"

Mayor Sullivan took advantage of the distraction to slip into the lobby of the building. Chase watched her glance back at the last moment before the door closed behind her. He could almost feel her sigh of relief at dodging Sylvia's inquisition.

The woman named Jessica moved closer, her gaze locked with Sylvia's. "I received a call late yesterday afternoon from the selection committee here in Garland. I was in New York, so I drove up this morning. What the hell is going on here, Sylvia? You told me landing this location was a cakewalk."

Chase watched Sylvia swallow hard, staring into the woman's face. "I… Uh… A call?"

"Yes."

Sylvia glanced from him to the woman named Jessica and back again. He nailed it. The woman was Sylvia's boss. "We need to talk, Jessica."

"Yes, we do."

Chase took a step toward the women. "Perhaps I can help clear things up."

Jessica turned. Chase put out his hand. "Chase Ellis, Ellis Locations, Inc."

She sneered. "Ah. The competition."

Sylvia pushed forward. "Chase, I need to talk with Jessica alone. If you don't mind." She grasped Jessica's elbow to lead her away from Chase, but the woman stood solidly still on the sidewalk, eyeing him.

"Of course." Chase turned slightly. "Catch up later?"

Sylvia didn't answer him right away, her focus on Jessica. Then she distractedly said, "I don't know, Chase." She tugged at Jessica again, who then took a step toward Chase, pulling out of Sylvia's grasp.

Jessica eyeballed him. "On second thought, perhaps let's just cut to the chase… Chase. You no doubt already know why I'm here." She turned to Sylvia. "And I suppose you do too. Why didn't you call me the second you learned what happened?"

Sylvia's face fell, her gaze fixed on Jessica. Her mouth opened and closed, but no words came out. She looked stunned, frustrated, and confused all at the same time. "Wait." She put up a hand and closed her eyes. "Just wait. This is all moving too fast. What is it you think you know, Jessica? I've not been told anything officially yet."

Jessica stared at her. Chase could feel the intensity between them and felt bad for Sylvia. He had to intervene.

"The official announcement is tomorrow morning," he offered.

Sylvia's boss shifted her gaze. "You don't know?"

"Know what?" He shrugged.

"The committee had an emergency meeting yesterday. Someone was ill, having surgery or something, so they met early. They awarded the permits to your company, Chase. You stole the location from the hometown girl who guaranteed me she had this deal in the bag from the get-go." Her gaze slowly shifted to Sylvia. "You lied to me."

Sylvia stepped forward. "Oh no. I did not lie. Yes, I was

very confident that I would land it. But I never guaranteed it. And I definitely didn't lie."

"You practically guaranteed it. I believe your words were something like, 'I'm going to hand Garland to you wrapped up with a Christmas bow and delivered by Santa himself.' Right?"

Sylvia shook her head rapidly. "That was just a way to say I was confident I could deliver. I didn't mean it as a promise or a guarantee. I swear, Jessica. I did my best work. This was a case of timing and…" She looked at Chase, and his heart fell a little at the heartbreak he saw in her eyes. "And competition."

Crossing her arms over her chest, Jessica glared at Sylvia, then rotated to stare at Chase. "Congratulations, Mr. Ellis. Be sure and send me your resume by the end of the week."

Confused, Chase jerked his head a bit. "What?"

"What?" That came from Sylvia, her face drawn into a scowl.

"I don't understand," he added.

Jessica stepped closer. "I'm hiring. Looking for a new location contractor." She then turned to Sylvia. "Because you, my dear, are fired. Good luck with your career, because you'll need it. You'll never work in LA again."

Chase stood stunned, shocked, and speechless. He watched Jessica turn and walk down the sidewalk, get into a luxury sedan and back out of the parking spot. After a moment, he swiveled to look at Sylvia, who stood glaring at him.

"You!" she shouted, pushing at his chest, her eyes filling with tears. "This is all your fault. You got what you wanted." She snorted in a sob. "Now get out of my way. I never want to see you again. And get out of my town!"

CHAPTER NINE

Sylvia spun around and hurried through the town hall door. Her mind was racing. There had to be a way to change the council's decision. Liz could help—after all, she was the mayor. The heavy door swung shut behind her, and she glanced at Chase and Jessica talking. His hands moved as quickly as his words. Sylvia paused. It felt like a lifetime since she stood in a parking lot, kissing him, and even though he refused her proposal, she still wanted to be with him. Damn, he was the tinsel on her Christmas tree. She felt shiny and bright standing beside him. He pointed toward her, and Jessica kept shaking her head. Sylvia knew there was no changing Jessica's mind.

Sylvia watched a minute more before she strode down the hallway. The heels on her sandals clicked on the marble floor, echoing in the silence. Each department had their doors closed. When she reached the mayor's door, she pressed her hand against her rolling stomach and walked inside. This was it, her last chance to get the permit.

The receptionist lifted his eyes to meet her. "May I help you?"

She noticed his nameplate. "Hello, Treavor. I'd like to see Mayor Sullivan. I'm Sylvia Moore."

"Do you have an appointment, Ms. Moore?"

"No. We were talking outside and got interrupted. I'm sure she has a busy schedule. I won't take much of her time."

Treavor pushed back from the desk and gestured to a red leather wingback chair across the room. "Have a seat and let me see if she has some time." He tapped on the door and disappeared inside.

Sylvia sat down and tried to clear her head. Instead, she kept rehearsing what else she could say to plead her case. One thing she knew—next time she wouldn't be so cavalier about securing a location. If she could get the permit, Jessica would reinstate her job.

Closing the door, Treavor came out of Liz's office, his face devoid of expression. Sylvia stood and approached his desk, the strap of her handbag twisted in her hands.

"Mayor Sullivan asked if you could come back. She has some things she must attend to first, but she can spare a few minutes for you around ten."

She exhaled. "I'll be here, and thank you, Treavor." Feeling more hopeful than when she came in, she walked out of the building. Glancing around, she didn't see Jessica or Chase out front, and the sidewalk was empty. Unsure where to go next, she crossed the street to the gazebo. Her anger hadn't kicked in yet, and who should she be angry with? Chase for doing his job better than she did? Jessica for butting her nose in and coming up here when she was already in the loop on what the council had decided? Or did she need to look at her actions and put the blame where it should be, on her own shoulders?

She acknowledged all Chase did was pursue a great filming location, but couldn't he have looked at the other options? Would it have killed him? A flicker of annoyance flared, but she tamped it back down. Her cheeks grew damp, and she wiped them with the back of her hand. Through her tears, she saw Chase jogging in her direction. Her heart ticked up, and she sat up a little straighter, trying to look like she hadn't been crying.

"I've been looking for you." He dropped onto the bench next to her, not quite touching. "I can understand if you never want to talk to me again. I didn't want you to get fired. If I had known, I would have done things differently."

She gave him a side-eye as her heart hammered in her chest. Just being close to him made her not care about the permit.

He continued. "I never dreamed that you'd get fired if you lost out on Garland."

She tore her gaze from the scruff of his beard and met his eyes. "I'm sure she doesn't mean it. Jessica's always had a hot temper." But in her heart, she knew she would never work for Jessica again.

Clasping and unclasping his hands, he leaned forward and handed her a piece of paper. She noted it wasn't folded and he must have read it based on the bereft expression on his face. "I'm sorry."

Consider this your notice that our contract is void. I'll pay the severance as stated. Don't contact me, or I will let others in the industry know you're unreliable. Jessica Griffin.

She crumpled the paper in her hand. "Well, that was to the point and final." She scanned the park, taking in the booths set up for the festival's grand finale tonight. "I guess I'll check out of the inn and stop to see my family before taking off."

"Just like that," he demanded. "You're giving up your company, your reputation?"

"What's the point? I was fired. I needed that contract to bridge me until I got the next one. Who knows, if Jessica follows through on her threat and places a few calls to any producers, my business may suffer irreparable damage. I'll be relegated to low-budget flicks and barely eke out a living."

Sylvia knew that snapping at Chase would not solve her

problem. What she needed was a solution and fast to keep her company from becoming dried out like a Christmas tree in January.

Chase reached for her hand, and she noticed he stopped himself. "I'll tell the board and Jessica that I withdraw my application. They'll have to give you the permit."

She shook her head. Not that she didn't appreciate the offer, but even if the board changed their minds, she knew Jessica and she'd never change hers. End of story.

"Don't. We don't need to implode both our companies over this." She got to her feet and stuck out her hand. "It's been nice getting to know you, but I'm gonna take off. I have a career to salvage and just a word of advice."

Chase cocked an eyebrow.

She continued. "If you decide to work with Jessica, watch every single syllable you say, as you heard earlier. She takes everything literally."

He clasped her hands, and the warmth radiated to her core. And this was just one more reminder of why she needed to go. She could never be with Chase Ellis; they would always be rivals in business. When he didn't let go, she glanced at their hands, and he released hers.

"See you around, Chase."

As she walked away, she wanted him to call out and stop her, ask her to stay in Garland. But she couldn't help but wonder if the spark between them was more than just leftover tension from their situation. He didn't. She had her answer, and now her temper spiked. It had been a game to him, but she wouldn't give him the satisfaction of watching her pick up the cookie crumbs of her life.

The bell on the door to Krissy's jingled when she walked in

after making a detour to see Liz. Thankfully, the shop was mostly empty, as the working crowd had come and gone.

Krissy flung a towel over one shoulder. "What's wrong? You look like someone just destroyed your life."

"Chase Ellis got my contract, and I got fired, and my entire career could be over with just a few phone calls."

Krissy pulled out a chair and nudged Sylvia to sit down. "I'll get coffee."

Sylvia set her handbag on the extra chair and turned away from the window. She didn't need anyone passing by, watching her cry into her coffee cup.

Two mugs clattered on the tabletop, and Krissy filled them to the rim with piping hot coffee. It was just what she needed.

"Tell me everything."

Sylvia took a sip and set the mug aside. "Yesterday, I came up with a brilliant idea. Chase could go to a neighboring town, like Grace Cove, and request a permit for his movie. I met him for a drink to give him my notes."

"I love Grace Cove. That's an excellent Plan B. Was he receptive?"

"He took the folder but—"

"Did you argue?" Krissy leaned forward and placed a comforting hand on Sylvia's arm.

Should she tell Krissy everything? Why not? She already wished things were different. Maybe sharing what had happened would help her forget about his lips on hers. "We kissed."

Jaw dropped and eyes wide, Krissy stared at her. "Like a sweet little kiss or the heart-thumping kind?"

"The second." She shrugged. "I drove around before going back to the inn. I saw him again. This time there was zero kissing, and he agreed to look over my ideas. When I went to bed, I hoped that he'd see reason, withdraw, and I'd get the permits. Jessica would be happy, and everything would be fine."

"Okay, sounds promising."

"Until this morning, and I find out from my uncle that Chase is getting the permits and I'm out of luck. Then, I went to the town hall to talk to the mayor and ask her to intervene on my behalf. Liz Sullivan and I were friends back in the day. But as we were talking on the sidewalk, Jessica showed up and fired me and then offered Chase a job. *My job*." Then she remembered he didn't turn down Jessica's off-the-cuff offer. Would he actually work for her?

Krissy's hand flew to her mouth. "Please tell me you're joking. Chase didn't strike me as the guy who would backstab anyone. He's always been nice when I've seen him here and around town."

With a snort, Sylvia said, "You've known him a week, not a lot to judge a man."

Tapping the tabletop with her fingernail, she said, "I'll have you know I'm good at reading people, and I would never have pegged him as a sneak."

"It doesn't matter now. I'm going to pack up my things and stop to see my family. Then head back to Los Angeles to see if I have a career left. Jessica is one tough woman in this business, and her word carries a lot of clout."

"What about Chase? I've seen you with him, and you two have undeniable chemistry. Are you interested in seeing where it could go? I haven't seen you look at anyone like that. Ever."

"Krissy, he didn't care what happened to me, that I'll become a pariah in a tight-knit industry. As someone who has paid their dues for years, I thought I had reached the next plateau and I could get another leg up securing this deal. Jessica had more movies that I know I would have been the ideal location scout. Chase took that away from me this week, and especially earlier today." She shook her head, almost to the point of making herself dizzy.

She smacked the tabletop. "I'm so done with Chase, and I

don't care how attracted I am to him. I could never be with anyone who would step into my shoes after I was ripped out of them."

The door opened.

Chase walked through.

Sylvia opened her mouth, and the snark just fell out. "Are you here to add salt to my coffee, or have you done enough for today?"

Chase's brow furrowed. "What's going on? An hour ago, you shook my hand, and we seemed to part as friends."

She crossed her arms over her chest, and Krissy pushed back her chair, making a quick escape to the kitchen without so much as a word.

"I realized you got everything you wanted and more. Should I just hand over all my contracts now and make it easier for you to take over the rest of my business?"

Sparks flashed from Chase's dark eyes. "Darlin', I don't know what happened between the gazebo and here, but we need to get a few things straight." He sat down after turning the chair around. "I'm not here to steal your clients. I'm here for you."

EPILOGUE

Five Months Later

Sylvia got out of the passenger seat and stretched her arms over her head. She smiled over the hood of the car at Chase, who was working the kinks out of his lower back. Driving from California had been a great idea to spend quality time together. He said, "All that windshield time is rough on the back and butt."

She gestured to Holly Hill Inn, decked out in Christmas wreaths and bows. "We're here, where it began."

Chase slid his sunglasses to rest on the top of his head, his dark hair poking out around them, his deep-brown eyes twinkling. "Where's all the snow? We're in New England, and I've seen the postcards. Heck, I've even made a movie here. It's in the rule book."

"Patience, love. We have a week until Christmas, and it will snow. Or maybe we can use movie magic to get it." She closed her car door and hurried around the front of the vehicle, pulling him into her arms. "You'll see what Christmas is like in Garland, and Charmington, and Grace Cove...." She shivered as his kiss warmed her all the way to the tips of her toes.

She looked up when the door banged. Kat strode across the front porch as she wiped her hands on a towel. "I like seeing two of my favorite people in love."

She closed the space between them and wrapped her arms around them, giving them a tight squeeze. "Does the family know you've arrived?"

Sylvia shook her head. "My folks are in town, and I thought we'd surprise them tonight at the town square when they're caroling."

Kat's eyes sparkled. "Good idea. Now get inside, and I'll fix you a snack. Unless you plan to pop into The Evergreen first?" She looked from Sylvia to Chase.

"We don't want to take any chances. We're going to hang out here until tonight." She gave Kat a long look, knowing how talk started in small towns. "You haven't mentioned that we booked a room, have you?"

She zipped her finger across her lip. "Not a peep out of me, and I made sure Dylan knew it was top secret." She pointed to the back of the vehicle. "Get your bags and meet me in the kitchen."

When Kat had gone inside, Chase picked up Sylvia's left hand and kissed the protruding bump on her glove-covered hand. "Do you think she suspects the real reason we're here?"

"Not a chance, and I can't wait to share our exciting news."

"Our engagement or the new company we've formed?" She stood on her tiptoes and brushed her lips over his, looking deep into his eyes.

He said, "That we share every aspect of our lives."

Sylvia sighed and grazed her lips over his again. "Love, business, life… I'm all yours, Chase Ellis. Always."

"And forever," he murmured.

The End… Hi! It's Lucinda and Maddie. We hope you loved reading *Christmas in July* as much as we enjoyed writing this free gift for you! We absolutely adore the Christmas town of Garland and have more books available for you in our Garland worlds.

Look for more Grace Cove books from Lucinda, and Charmington books from Maddie. Scroll on for more information!

FROM LUCINDA RACE

More Small-Town Christmas Books!

Holiday Hearts - A Boxset
Holly Berries and Hockey Pucks
A Secret Santa Christmas

FROM MADDIE JAMES

The Charmington Books

Home for Christmas
Miracle at Holly Hill Inn

The Last Christmas at Holly Hill Inn
Charming the Prince

ABOUT THE AUTHORS

Lucinda Race

Award-winning and best-selling author Lucinda Race has been captivated by stories for as long as she can remember. A lifelong reader who fell head over heels for cozy mysteries and heartfelt romances as a young girl, she now brings that same magic to the pages of her own books.

Stories Filled with Heart, Hope, and a Hint of Mystery

Although her writing career began in nonfiction, storytelling always called her back home. Today, she delights readers with beloved series like the **McKenna Family Romance** and the **Paranormal Cozy Nook Bookstore Mysteries**, where charming small towns, lovable characters, and page-turning twists keep readers coming back for more.

Whether crafting a swoon-worthy romance or a clever cozy mystery, Lucinda writes the kinds of stories she loves to read—**uplifting tales that leave readers smiling long after the final page.**

Now with over 40 books published, she's living her dream and loves connecting with readers at LucindaRace.com

Maddie James

Fiction with a pulse—small towns, big drama, perhaps a dash of danger, and a guaranteed satisfying ending.

Maddie James writes emotional, page-turning love stories rooted in small-town life, often with a twist of suspense, a dash of danger, or even a ghost or two. Her books span contemporary westerns, romantic suspense, and paranormal romance, and feature cowboys, chefs, spunky heroines, and the kind of heroes you don't forget.

With over 70 titles published, Maddie has built a loyal base of readers who love strong women, rugged men, and small towns with big secrets. Whether you're looking for a standalone escape or a bingeable series, there's a Maddie James romance waiting to sweep you off your feet.

As Madeleine Jaimes, she writes women's fiction with powerful themes, layered characters, and small-town stories where every woman's journey matters. Learn more at www.maddiejamesbooks.com

www.ingramcontent.com/pod-product-compliance
Lightning Source LLC
LaVergne TN
LVHW041130150826
845673LV00007B/2253

* 9 7 9 8 2 1 5 6 8 1 6 8 8 *